Sawyer, Iris & Isaiah,

May your life be filled with great adventures, deep friendships, and silly humor!

Hoagie
& Katie

Hoagie & Katie

RIO KOVIAK

LUMADIX PRESS

Published by
Lumadix Press / Rio Koviak / *the*BookDesigners
www.riokoviak.com

Paperback ISBN 13: 978-0-9981647-2-4
Hardcover ISBN 13: 978-0-9981647-0-0
eBook ISBN: 978-0-9981647-1-7

Excerpt From: Rio Koviak. "Hoagie & Katie." iBooks.

Cover and interior layout designed by *the*BookDesigners
www.bookdesigners.com

Printed in USA by Ingram Spark
www.ingramspark.com

To my children, who claimed they couldn't
go to sleep without a story with funny voices.

And to my Love, for planting the seed,
convincing me, and believing in me.

—RMK

Contents

1
FOREST FREEDOM

The ball rolled…and rolled…and rolled. The forest floor was bumpy, littered with twigs, pebbles, and dry, crunchy leaves. Hoagie noticed that his door was rattling a little; with one final roll, the door snapped wide open. He stumbled out, doing a little somersault, and his beady eyes blinked in the bright sunlight coming through the tall trees. The mossy earth and pokey twigs felt strange on his tiny feet. And everything seemed so colorful somehow. The greens were greener, the blues were bluer, and the browns were almost reddish. Also, it was cooler outside than in his big plastic purple ball. And the air! It smelled so sweet, and wet, and oddly *fresh*. He could actually take deep breaths without his lungs hurting for once. For a few moments, Hoagie simply sat there gulping and allowing his body to fill up with this sweet new air.

Hoagie decided to be daring and step away from the protection of his hamster ball. He slowly put one teensy toe out to touch the soft ground… pat, pat, pat. The earth felt very cool. Again, he stepped out even further…

pat, pat, patty-pat. Suddenly, he heard a small crack behind him, and he ran like the wind! Huffing and puffing, he raced toward the nearest tree he could find. He hid under a log, sticking his nose out and sniffing the air, wondering what could've made the terrible noise that spooked him. Hoagie wasn't used to the outdoors and all the "outdoor" noises and smells, so he didn't really know what was normal around here. He was only allowed outside if he was in his quiet, safe hamster ball. For a moment, he just sat there, shivering with fright. He thought, *Oh! What did I do?! Why did I roll so far away from my humans? And what in the world is wiggling next to my foot?!*

It was a long, squiggly, slimy thing, and it didn't look like it had eyes!! Hoagie stared as it slowly slithered towards him. He tried to scoot out of the way, but there wasn't much room under the log. It came closer, stopped, then randomly changed direction. Suddenly, the thingie curled up and stopped moving altogether. Hoagie was relieved. He sniffed the thing. It smelled weird. On the second sniff, Hoagie's nose accidentally touched it, and the skinny thing moved a little. Hoagie jumped out of the way! Without warning, it began to burrow *into* the ground! And then...it wasn't there at all! It completely disappeared!

Hoagie became curious and began to dig where the creature had disappeared. In no time at all, he had dug a small hole in the dirt and found the creature with his paw. It felt squishy, and for some reason, it felt oddly like food. He took his foot off the thing and licked his toe. Sure enough, the smell and taste of his own toe made him feel hungry. Without even thinking, he snatched the thing up, and gobbled it down. *Oh, so tasty!!!* he sang

to himself. Hoagie had never eaten a worm before, and eating it had made him realize just how hungry he really was. He felt like he wanted to search for more fat, juicy worms; so he did. After he stuffed himself, Hoagie was in a food daze, and all he wanted to do was groom himself and rest his roly-poly body somewhere safe and warm. So he spied a cozy spot, and closed his little peepers.

After a while, Hoagie woke up to some super loud sniffing. It sounded like a small vacuum was being turned on and off, over and over again. He jolted up and looked around, but everything was different. It was no longer daylight outside, but instead, blacker than black! Hoagie had never seen darkness quite like this before, as there had always been a night-light in his human's room. It was rather spooky. Oh how Hoagie missed sleeping in his cage with the warm night-light on in his human's room! He didn't have time to think about that, though because he heard the sniffing sound again, and it sounded like it was getting closer. He shuffled out from his resting spot into a little clearing, and when Hoagie looked around, he quickly forgot about the threatening sniff, because he couldn't believe his little beady black eyes! There was a bunch of shining sparkling things up in the clear night sky that seemed to be winking at him. And there were so many of them!! The sight of these tiny bright lights took his breath away, and when he found his voice again, he whispered, "Hey! You look so friendly twinkling like that! Hello? Hey you!!"

Before the twinkly things had a chance to answer, Hoagie heard that sniffing sound again! "Sniff, sniff, sniiiiiiiif!!"

Hoagie tried to hide under a branch, but when he backed up, he bumped into something…and it was big! All of the hair on his round body stood on end, and he was afraid to even turn around! All of a sudden, he felt hot air on his back, and heard the hugest sniff in his entire life!

2
COUSINS

Hoagie couldn't help but squeal, "Oh my day-day, oh my day-day!" He heard an even a bigger squeal than his own, right behind him! When Hoagie finally turned around, he saw, to his great surprise, that crouching behind him was another hamster, the most gigantic hamster he had ever seen! Or was it a guinea pig? But even guinea pigs weren't that huge! It was at least four times his size, and, like him, was shivering with fear. They both sat staring at each other, their chests heaving frantically up and down, faster and faster. After much staring, the two of them started sniffing one another, and Hoagie realized that the loud sniffs he had heard earlier were actually coming from this giant hamster / guinea pig thingie.

"Hey, *you're* the loud sniffer!" Hoagie called up. The large hamster simply kept staring, and sniffing.

Hoagie repeated, "I *SAID*, you're the loud sniffer!" The strange hamster's eyes went blink, blink-blink.

Hmmmm, wondered Hoagie, *I guess the thingie can't hear, or speak, or sump'em*.

"I thought I smelled something rather…stinky and small. Don't mean to be rude, of course," said the stranger suddenly.

"What?!" Hoagie blurted out. He certainly didn't appreciate being called "small," or "stinky", for that matter. Once he took a quick whiff of himself, though, he had to admit, he actually was a little smelly.

Hoagie admitted, "Yeah, okay. I get it. I smell a tad bit ripe, and I'm sure there are reasons for that. But, one thing I'm not is 'small.' You just happen to be ridiculously big, is all! Did you eat too much food, or sump'em?"

"The real question is: why are so *you* much *tinier* than me?" replied the larger hamster. "Are you a wee baby? I think I was bigger than you when I was *born*…but I wouldn't really know that, 'cuz I don't remember being born, of course…but I'm only five months old myself, and lookie how big I am compared to you!"

"I'm certainly not a baby, that's for sure!" Hoagie responded. "I just had my second birthday recently, and was given presents and everything 'cuz my people love me so much. I think I've always been this size (which is a perfect size, by the way). Yeah, if I was any bigger, I wouldn't fit into my cage, or my fun rolling ball!" Hoagie huffed.

"Cage? Rolling ball? I don't know what those things are 'cuz we don't have anything like that in my village…with my family." Suddenly, the big hamster started wiping its eyes, and Hoagie noticed a large tear trickling down its face.

"Ooh…um…What's happening?" Hoagie asked uncomfortably. Hoagie never had to comfort anyone before and felt awkward in this situation.

"Oh, I got lost from my family somehow, and I've been out here, all alone, for many days I think," sniffled the big hamster.

"Being alone ain't so bad," Hoagie said. "I like being alone…I'm used to it and wouldn't want it any other way! I rolled out too far in my ball and I also got lost from my family, but I don't care! I'm thinking I can have myself a great adventure! I'm Hoagie, by the way."

"My name's Katie, and it sure feels good knowing I'm not the only lost capybara out here. What village are you from?"

"Uh, excuse me? Cappy-*what*? Cappy-*who*?" Now Hoagie was totally confused. Maybe he was wrong all along; maybe this thing wasn't an overgrown guinea pig or hamster at all.

"Capybara, silly! That's what we are, didn't you know? Your family never told you what you are?"

"I don't know anything about this so-called 'capybara' stuff, but I *do* know that I'm a hamster; in fact, everybody knows that!"

Hoagie was beginning to get a little annoyed with this creature, so he turned away and decided to walk back to his ball. Katie waddled alongside him clumsily. When they both got to the ball, Hoagie tried to get back inside, but he noticed that the door had broken completely off. He was so frustrated that he couldn't help letting out a worried little squeak.

Katie began making little chirping sounds in order to comfort poor Hoagie. She got closer, and before they knew what was happening, both of them were cuddling up and squeaking softly together, and that is when their friendship began.

3
HOAGIE'S FIRST SWIM

Once Katie and Hoagie became friends, they found out that they weren't the same kind of animal at all. Hoagie was a fluffy cream, black, and tan teddy-bear hamster, and Katie was a Central American capybara. Katie lived in the forest with her parents and fifteen relatives: brothers, sisters, aunts, cousins, and uncles. Her most favorite things in the whole world were napping in the sun, swimming in the lake, and eating mangoes.

"Whoa! That's kinda crazy, living with all those people! I don't know if I could handle all that noise! And sharing all your food too?! No thanks! That would be a super-duper drag!"

"Nah, it's not so bad. I like having a lot of people to play with and talk to. And there's plenty to eat 'cuz grass, plants, and tree bark are everywhere! Sometimes though, to be honest"—Katie looked around to make sure no one was listening—"I don't like to share the berries, and I absolutely *hate* sharing the mango fruit! It was all because of the mango that I got lost....I wanted it all for myself," Katie admitted.

"Speaking of secrets, can I tell you one? I ate something totally squishy and salty today. And I think I must be weird, 'cuz…I liked it. In fact, I loved it!"

"Ewww! That *is* kinda weird. But I've eaten things I'm not so proud of too; like all the time. So I'm thinking it's probably normal, and you shouldn't be embarrassed." The two friends laughed at themselves. "So, where do you live all alone, being able to eat all the food to yourself?" Katie continued.

"I live in what's called a 'house.' That's a big indoor place with lots of rooms to do different things: like eating, sleeping, relaxing, and even…going potty!"

"Now, *that* is the weirdest thing you've said all day!" gasped Katie.

"And I'm not totally alone. I have 'humans.' They're big, hairless creatures who walk on their two hind legs. They live with me, feed me, and sing to me."

"Are you the king where you live, even though you are so tiny?"

"Now, why do you always have to bring up the fact that I'm smaller than you are?" Hoagie asked irritably. "No, I'm no king, but it's not because I'm small. One of the big humans is like a king, I guess. And there's another sorta-big human that's kinda like a queen, and then there are two smaller humans. Those are the ones who take care of me. See, I'm what you call 'a pet' 'cuz they pet me all the time. And they hold me, talk to me in baby voices, and love me. The little girl-human is the one who sings to me at night before she goes to bed 'cuz she loves me the most." Hoagie sighed, feeling a little homesick again.

"Sounds to me like you're at least a prince! Funny, you don't look—" Katie suddenly stopped, looked around, and began sniffing. Hoagie also froze and sniffed the air.

"Did you hear that?" Katie whispered. Hoagie nodded quietly. Slowly, the two of them edged closer together, rumps touching. Both their noses sniffed in opposite directions.

"I really can't see too far out," grumbled Hoagie, who was trying his hardest to listen where the sound had come from.

"Me neither, but I've smelled that smell before, even though I've actually never *seen* what that smell is. But if it made my daddy bark and my uncles whistle for us to jump into the lake, it can't be good." Katie shuddered. She was getting very nervous now, which made Hoagie nervous, and when Hoagie got nervous, he made a bunch of noise.

"Oh my day—" he began, but Katie quickly cut him off.

"No, don't do that!" hissed Katie. "Be quiet, silly! You're gonna give us away!!" and just as she finished those words, they saw a streak of spots rush by.

"Run!!!" Katie yelled. Hoagie tried to keep up as best he could, and ran in a zig-zag pattern. He could barely hear Katie over the loud thumping of his own heart. Katie was squealing, "Oh, my gosh! Where is that lake?"

Almost out of breath, Hoagie panted, "Lake? Wait! I don't think I can swim! I've never done it before, and the few times my girl gave me a bath, I hated it. It freaked me out and I got sick!" Just the thought of plunging into the icy water made Hoagie shiver more than ever.

Katie turned on her heel, staring at him with wide eyes. Hoagie took a step back when she barked, "Listen up, 'cuz I'm not gonna say it again. We gotta find the lake! I bet this thing hates water more than you do, so stop your whining and hop on my back! You said you weren't a prince, so don't start acting like one

now!!" Katie sat down and pointed to her back, and, without a thought, Hoagie did as he was told. He climbed up her scratchy back and held on for dear life!

"Let's get outta here!" Hoagie yelled, and in an instant, Katie waddled so fast, she probably could've won a medal.

Pretty soon, they could see the edge of the water in the distance. They were so close! All of a sudden, a big spotted cat jumped out in front of them, blocking off the water. It growled and hissed, showing off its pointy fangs. It looked like it was going to pounce on them!

"Oh my day-daaay!!!" screamed Hoagie, clutching tightly to Katie's hair.

"And where do you think you're going, my little morsels?" hissed the spotted cat.

Katie was shivering so much she didn't think she would be able to stand much longer. Hoagie knew if she was too scared, they would never be able to make it to the lake. He also knew that if she couldn't swim, he wouldn't be able to go it alone. Hoagie never thought he'd want to be in water as much as he did right now.

Hoagie put on his most fancy and confident voice, announcing, "We're going to meet a few friends, you know—*a few hundred friends, actually*—at the waterfront for a little par-tee. They'd be absolutely delighted if you would join us."

"Oh nooo, you're not going anywhere," the spotted cat snickered. It wasn't easily fooled. It crept closer, still baring its teeth.

Katie slowly backed up and looked frantically around, wondering where they could hide. Meanwhile Hoagie was trying to figure out a master plan.

Hoagie crawled up near Katie's head and whispered, "Listen, can you grunt, bark, or do sump'em wild?"

Katie nodded slowly.

"Okay, you start barking, then. This will distract her, and then she won't notice me slide down your back, you see? I'll meet you by the water. I'm smaller than you are (as you keep pointing out), so I can run under things and squeeze through tight spaces. You ready?"

Katie nodded her head again.

"'K, on the count of three..."

"So, which one of you should I eat first?" asked the spotted cat. "The little one will be my snack, and the big one will be my lunch...or should I have the big one first and the plump one as my dessert? It's too hard to decide!"

The cat slinked even closer, and Hoagie whispered, "1...2...3...go!"

Katie made quite a show of loud barking, nodding her head up and down and shaking it side to side. She looked crazy! Meanwhile, Hoagie quickly crawled down her side, where the cat couldn't see him, and was able to get a good distance away.

He called out, "Hey, Dots! Yeah, you! Over here! If you can catch me, you can eat *me* first!"

And with that, Hoagie starting running in his zigzag fashion toward the water. This triggered the spotted cat to start the chase. Katie took one last look in Hoagie's direction, silently wishing him the best of luck, and started off at a jog, which quickly turned into a run. She even surprised herself at how speedy she could be; she didn't know she could run almost as fast as a small horse! In no time at all, she submerged herself in the water. Only her little ears, eyes, and nose were sticking out. She waited and waited. She was getting very worried for poor Hoagie.

It seemed to Katie that she had been waiting a lifetime when she finally spied something moving around in the tall grass. She saw the cat too, but it was further away. Katie decided to give a few short barks, and since Hoagie had such great hearing, he ran towards the lake where she was hiding. Unfortunately, the cat saw Hoagie too, and sprinted towards him. That cat was fast! It was gaining on him, and Hoagie's little legs were getting tired. Katie swam closer to the shoreline with her head sticking out of the water.

She called out, "Hurry! She's getting closer! Jump on my nose!!"

Hoagie could now feel the cat's breath near his back, and Hoagie made one final zigzag, then jumped onto Katie's nose.

As Katie started swimming away, the cat yelled, "Oh-ho! I'm an ocelot and I'm not afraid of water. In fact, it's a good day to go for a little swim!" and it jumped in the lake, with a loud splash.

Katie would have swum underwater to get away more easily, but she knew Hoagie probably didn't know how to hold his breath. Instead, she just swam as fast as she could with the top of her head peeking out. She quickly paddled out to the deepest part of the lake, where the ocelot wasn't willing to go. Katie finally turned around to watch the ocelot swim back to shore.

"Adios, Dots!" Hoagie called out.

Hoagie was happy that he wasn't the ocelot's meal, but he was still pretty terrified of being that far out in the water. Eventually, Katie found a safe place to get out of the lake. After they both shook themselves off, they started laughing and jumping for joy at their grand escape.

"Did you see Dots hiss when she saw your head sticking out of the water?" Hoagie laughed.

"Yeah! Did you see her turn around and make that ugly face and spit when you called her 'Dots'?"

"Yeah, that was great! Wow! I can't believe we got away! Hey, you're a great swimmer, by the way. Thanks for saving our lives," said Hoagie.

"It was nothing! Thanks for thinking of such a great plan! I was so worried she was going to gobble you up! I guess being small isn't that big of a deal after all, especially if you got good brains, and you can run the way you did," added Katie.

They continued to thank each other and relive their adventure, going over every detail they could remember. Eventually, they both realized one important thing…they were starving!

4
COTTON CANDY

Now, since both animals were comfortable being nocturnal (that means they liked being active at night), they ate most of their food in darkness. Katie stayed close to the lake and gobbled up water plants, while Hoagie went out on his own digging for more worms. He had finally gotten used to the total darkness of the forest sky.

"You should totally try eating some grass, Hoagie!" called out Katie, with her cheeks stuffed with food.

"Poochie!! That sounds ga-ross!" spat Hoagie.

"Hey, didn't your mama ever tell you it's rude to shut down a food before trying it first?"

"I don't actually remember having a mama, but I suppose I did once," replied Hoagie, lost in thought.

"Well, let's pretend I'm your mama, and I say, um-hum…" she cleared her throat and put on her best "mama" voice, "Try the grass, dear! Give it a chance!"

Since Hoagie was growing tired of digging for worms anyway, he went ahead and nibbled a blade of grass, and was surprised to find that the grass wasn't that bad after all. It did get caught between his teeth, which was rather annoying, but he could use that as a snack later on.

When the two friends were fully satisfied from eating, the sun began to peek out through the tops of the forest trees. They decided that it was time to start searching for Katie's family. Katie thought it would be a good idea to travel by water so that Dots or any other predators couldn't sniff them out. Hoagie, on the other hand, wasn't a big fan of that idea, so he proposed something else.

"Tell ya what I'm thinking…I can climb this here tree, and go from tree limb to tree limb, following you from up above. I think I can do it, if we don't go too far and take a few breaks along the way." Hoagie felt very proud of his tree-climbing abilities, and was eager to show off.

So their journey began, with Katie in the water and Hoagie in the trees. He had a rougher time than he had imagined, because the branches were so much thicker and bumpier than anything he had ever climbed in his cage back home. Plus, the branches had great big shiny green things that kept poking him in the face. It was also difficult to climb and watch Katie at the same time. There were many times when Hoagie almost fell off a limb because he was looking at her instead of where he was going. His little legs were beginning to get sore, so he finally slumped down on a long green tree limb to take a short rest. Hoagie was looking out towards the water when he saw it.

This was the second time in his life Hoagie couldn't believe his eyes! The sky was filled with pink, fluffy things (like the sticky stuff the children ate after coming back from a carnival), and the water was also pinkish. Beyond

the lake, there seemed to be a smudge of golden fire, and the rest of the sky appeared purple. Hoagie felt that the sky was magical, and was completely enchanted by the sight of his first sunrise. Hoagie just sat staring with his mouth and eyes wide open.

It wasn't long before Katie noticed Hoagie wasn't on the move, and called up to him.

"Hoagie! Where are ya? Are you alright?"

Hoagie was still under the sky's spell, and murmured dreamily. "Yep…just resting by all these shiny green things up here…feeling cozy…"

"Feeling cozy, are you? It's one thing to take a rest, but feeling cozy? That's a little much! We have to get a move on!" Katie thought for a second. "What shiny green things?" She thought a little more. "Oh, those are leaves, silly! Trees make them."

"Yeah, well, …those 'leaves' keep poking me in the face and butt—it's like they got something against me! And these huge branches! I've never seen branches like this where I come from! And I didn't know branches could be green and cool and soft, too…" Hoagie was getting ready to curl up, when he heard Katie scream from down below.

"No, Hoagie!! Get away from there, n-n-n-now!" she stammered.

"Why?" but before he could say another word, he suddenly felt the big "green branch" move underneath him.

"Hurry, Hoagie! It's a snake! Probably a v-v-viper!!" Katie was now out of the water, running towards Hoagie's tree. Hoagie didn't know what a snake was, but he could hear the terror in Katie's voice, so he didn't ask any more questions and ran straight down the tree trunk in that zigzag motion he was so good at.

Sure enough, once he got back down to the forest floor and looked up, he saw a thick, green, gigantic wormlike creature staring at him with red eyes. It was flicking its tongue out at him, too, which Hoagie didn't like one bit.

Now that Hoagie was safe, he felt more brave, and said, "Whatcha sticking your tongue at me for, huh? That's kinda bratty. I didn't do nothin' except sit on ya by accident! Jeez, you're so sensitive!"

Hoagie stuck his tongue out as well. But the snake kept sticking its tongue in and out…in and out, which seemed very strange. It even started to slither down the tree towards him, and it didn't look like it was in a playful mood at all! This made Hoagie feel very uncomfortable and unsafe again.

"Come here, butterball," it hissed. "You're so juicy and pretty, let me get a closer look at you…mmm?"

As soon as Hoagie heard that creepy voice, he hopped right on top of Katie's head and the two of them took to the water at once.

5
FEATHERS *to the* RESCUE

"That was a close call!" Katie huffed as she swam with Hoagie on top of her head. "You've gotta be careful out here 'cuz there are lots of predators that would love to eat you up. That's why family is so important: everyone can keep an eye out for each other."

"The only predator we had at my house was the big, dopey dog, but he was lazy, and harmless, and *cozy*. I had to watch out for the children and their friends—they were the wild ones!" Hoagie was starting to shiver because all the splashes of water were soaking him to the bone. He added, "And...did I hear that snake right? Did he say I was *pretty*?! Do you think I'm pretty?"

"Well, I'd definitely say you are 'different' looking...but in a good way, of course!" Katie changed the subject. "Is your house close by here, I wonder, 'cuz I've never seen anything like that around here; just wild nature. I'm sure your people are worried about you."

"I don't know...I have no idea where to look first. I do know that this isn't where the family normally lives; the family was just visiting this place because of some 'wildlife protection work', or sump'em like that. They could have already left by now, for all we know." Hoagie was beginning to miss his old life and humans again. He even kind of missed that big, dopey, slobbery dog, too.

"Okay, well, we'll just have to look for my family first, then...oh look! *They* might be able to help us!" The two friends came upon a huge flock of flamingos wading in the shallow end of the lake, searching for food in the mud. As soon as they approached, most of the flamingos got spooked and flew off.

"Hey! Where ya going? We're not gonna hurt you!" Hoagie called out. "My friend here might be big—gigantic even—but, trust me, she's very nice and gentle!" More birds flew away when Hoagie started speaking. While the flamingos were used to capybaras, none of them had ever seen a teddy-bear hamster before, and thought *Hoagie* was the weirdo!

Katie spoke gently to one of the younger, gray flamingos, "Excuse me, have you seen my herd, by any chance?"

The gray flamingo raised its beak from the mud to reply, "Um...no, I don't think so..."

"Have you heard any barking or other capybara-ish noises lately?" Katie continued.

"Well...we've only just got here, and *we* were making so much noise, I've almost gone deaf myself! But if we get real quiet, maybe we'll hear something," said the flamingo.

All three of them stood very still, and were very quiet. Holding their breaths, they looked around with their eyes blinking.

After a while, Hoagie said, "Jeez, this is ridiculous! How long we gonna

be quiet like this? I don't hear a thing except for my own growling stomach!"

"You're right, Hoagie. Let's keep going. Thanks for your help, mister." Katie started to sulk away.

The flamingo came towards her and said, "Maybe I can help by flying out a bit to see what I can see. And the name's Joe, Flamingo Joe," he added as he began to fly away.

"Thanks, Flamingo Joe! Wow! That was lucky, huh, Hoagie? I thought—hey, why are you dancing on my head like that?!" Katie tried to look up at Hoagie, but because he was on her head, she couldn't see him no matter how hard she tried. The truth was, Hoagie wasn't dancing at all, but was shivering like crazy.

"No, not dancing…ooo…ooh. I'm ju-u-u-ust a little cold, that's all." Hoagie sneezed.

"We got to get you back on land and in the sun pronto, buddy! Being cold isn't good for a tiny…uhhh, I mean, *smaller* creature like you." Since Katie was in the shallow end, she quickly found a sunny spot in the sand. "Curl up next to me, Hoagie. My big ole body will keep you warm until Flamingo Joe comes back."

Still shivering, Hoagie curled up next to Katie. She smiled, "See, sometimes it's good to be plump. It makes for some good, cozy cuddling." And within minutes, the two of them were snoozing like babies.

The two friends woke up to a bunch of loud squawking and looked up to see Flamingo Joe landing awkwardly near them. He told them that he had seen a large group of capybaras sunning and swimming around in the lake further

upstream. He also said there was a small island in the middle of the lake.

"And, you gotta watch where you step because there are dangerous, freaky froggies on that island!" Flamingo Joe warned.

"Freaky froggies?! You mean, little, *innocent* frogs?" Katie laughed. "You're not serious, are you? They can't eat us, silly; we're too big!"

"Yeah, and I'm not afraid of no froggies, anyway—freaky, or regular!" added Hoagie, who was feeling much better (and braver) now that he was nice and dry again.

"Naw, Capy, those froggies aren't 'innocent.' They have poison in their skin, and that's how they can hurt you! They can even kill you! So whatever you do, don't touch them!" Apparently, Flamingo Joe *was* serious.

"Man! You guys really do live in a dangerous world!" gasped Hoagie looking around nervously.

"Just watch out for them, that's all I'm saying. The daddies can be mean, but they'll leave you alone if you leave them alone." Flamingo Joe nodded upstream. "Go that way…and good luck!" and then he turned and flew back to his flock.

6

DART ISLAND

After much grooming and a light snack of grass, worms, and tiny berries, Hoagie and Katie figured they would travel by day so they could see things more clearly (and things would look less spooky, too). They would stick close to the shoreline in case they needed to make a quick getaway, waiting until the hottest part of the day to travel by water to get to the island.

They hiked as long as they had enough energy, and finally stopped to forage because their legs felt like wet noodles and their stomachs were growling like mad dogs. By midafternoon, they spied Dart Island. It didn't seem to be too far off for a good swimmer like Katie, and since it was already hot outside, they decided to swim for it.

Once they swam to the island, they stopped to groom and eat (of course), and began their difficult journey through the island to get to the other side where the herd of capybaras was supposed to be.

"Hey, Katie," Hoagie said. "Remember to watch out for those frogs, 'k?"

Katie chuckled. "I think Flamingo Joe was making a big deal outta nothing. I mean, really, why should we be afraid of froggies? Who cares if they have weird skin?"

"Oh my day-day! Isn't that one right over there?" gasped Hoagie, pointing at a small, colorful frog on a rock. The frog's body was red with black stripes and spots, and its legs were blue with black spots. It was actually quite beautiful, and both Hoagie and Katie found it hard to believe that something so amazing could be so dangerous.

"Hey there, little froggy. Can I just say that you are the most magnificent animal I've ever seen? A friend of mine said that you could hurt us, though. But you wouldn't do that, would you, pretty froggy?" Katie cooed.

The itty-bitty frog hopped a little closer to get a better look at the friends, and spoke in a croaky, ancient voice.

"Oh, no siree, I wouldn't hurt you. I'm an old timer, you see, and I just want to live peacefully and enjoy myself. I have no need to fight, and I certainly have no need to hurt anyone," said the frog.

Hoagie still wasn't totally convinced and whispered, "Just be careful, is all I'm saying. Remember what Joe said."

The old frog still had great hearing, and croaked softly, "Joe? I never met a 'Joe,' so I don't think I hurt him before...unless...it was that time I had a terrible itch on my back, and I rubbed myself on what I thought was a tree, but it ended up being a chameleon. It is true, though, that some poison dart frogs can be rather grouchy and ready for a fight...yes, sad, but true." The frog shook her head wearily.

Hoagie finally decided to trust the frog and said, "Alrighty. We'll believe you—even though we just met you and we could be falling into a trap!—and maybe you can help us. That's Katie over there, and I'm Hoagie. We're looking for Katie's family. Have you seen them anywhere?"

The frog's face crinkled up in thought once again, and she said, "Now that you mention it, I did hear some snorting noises and splashing in the lake, like there were animals playing in it. And I thought to myself, 'Who could be making all that ruckus?' Then I went closer to the water and when I looked up, I saw a gray flamingo flying overhead, and thought that was even stranger than the ruckus sounds, as I didn't even know that flamingos could fly! And then… what was I saying? Oh yes! Then I looked *in* the water, and sure enough, there was a bunch of animals that look just like…you!" and she pointed at Katie.

"Oh, hurray!! Where were they?" asked Katie excitedly.

"On the other side of the island. They seemed like a lively bunch, too. Almost like they were having a bit of a party."

"A party?" asked Katie.

"Yes, with the way they were frolicking about in the water, and playing chase with each other! It seemed like everyone was having a grand ole time!"

Katie muttered, "Oh, really? Even the older, bigger capybaras?"

"Oh yes…everyone was very playful and in good spirits," said the frog.

"Well…thanks a lot…uh…" They never knew the frog's name, and now it seemed kind of awkward to ask.

Thankfully, the frog answered quickly, "Felipa. And I hope you find your festive family, little one. It's a dangerous world out here without your tribe's protection. And remember, always listen to your elders, children. The old folks have been around the longest, and can always give you the best advice."

Softly, Katie replied, "Thanks a lot, Felipa. Good luck with having that peaceful life you've been looking for." Katie slowly turned and waddled back towards the shore, her head hanging low.

"Yeah, and thanks for not rubbing your toxic body all over us!" added Hoagie. He darted off to join Katie, chatting away, "That frog sure was nice, huh? She didn't seem aggressive at all. And she was so helpful! But boy, she was quite the talker…" Hoagie was getting out of breath trying to catch up with Katie, who was practically trotting.

Hoagie gasped, "Hey, wait up, already! What's the rush? Why you even

going this way, Katie? Felipa said the other side of the island."

Katie was in no mood to talk. "I just want to be alone right now, Hoagie, if that's okay," she called over her shoulder. She slowly slipped into the lake.

"Oh, all right. I guess I'll just hang out here all by my lonesome self, then. Yeah, I like being alone anyway. In fact, I love it! I'm an only child, you know. Did I ever tell you that?" Hoagie looked around and found he was talking to himself, as Katie had submerged herself underwater. A little embarrassed, he did what he always did when there was nothing else to do: he groomed himself, and ate something (of course).

It didn't take too long before Hoagie was full, and he began to look around for Katie. He found her down the shoreline, sunning herself on the sand. Hoagie snuggled up to her and asked, "Should I get you sump'in? Are you in need of a certain grass, or…I know! That fruit that you like that starts with 'MMM'?"

"Mango," Katie said softly.

"Yeah, that! I wonder, do you think I'd like it?" Katie still didn't answer.

"What does it look like?" Hoagie continued. He began to think of all sorts of delicious fruit-like things with bright colors; his mouth started to water.

Katie finally spoke up. "No, I don't want a mango right now, Hoagie, I just want to sleep or something. I don't want to think or talk about anything right now." Katie closed her eyes.

Finally Hoagie realized something was not right with Katie. Hoagie thought she seemed rather bummed out. Usually she was pretty perky, and he was surprised that she wasn't super excited knowing that her family was nearby.

"Are you not feeling well, Kate?" he asked gently. Katie still didn't seem to want to chat. So, to help turn her mood around, Hoagie did something he had never done in public before. Hoagie decided to do a little song and dance routine.

First, he cleared his throat. "Eh-hem!! Heeemmm!" Then he began in a shaky, strained voice, "Skitta-ma-rinky dinky-dink, skitta-ma-rinky doo!" He started dancing on his hind legs, holding a big leaf in his hand, as though it was a top hat. He continued this way for a bit until Katie giggled when she saw how ridiculous Hoagie looked, and how horrible he sounded."What the…?!" she laughed harder and longer than she had in a very long time.

Hoagie beamed! He was so glad that his song and wonderful voice made Katie forget her troubles for a moment. He laughed at himself, though, when he saw Katie staring at him like he had gone cuckoo.

"You know, it's just a little ditty I picked up around the kids; they couldn't get enough of that song. You like it? You gotta admit, it's quite spunky." Hoagie rattled on for a while, then finally asked, "So, what's wrong, Katie? You seem down."

Katie sighed, "I thought my herd was gonna be worried about me… I thought they were gonna be sad that I've gone missing. And when Felipa said they were all having a great time playing and splashing about, it's like they didn't even notice that I had left at all! It's like they don't even care about me anymore!" Katie began to cry great, big tears. Unfortunately for Hoagie, her salty tears came down on him like rain.

"There, there! C'mon, you don't really believe that, do you? You know

you're a great person. A *kind* person. I'm sure your whole family loves and misses you! We've only been gone a couple of days, I think, and they probably thought you were with them when they crossed over to this island."

"But someone should have noticed by now! They should've sent a search party or something!" Katie sobbed.

"Okay…let me ask you a question: is this the first time you've wandered off looking for mangos by yourself?"

"Well, no…not really. It's something I always get in trouble for, actually. But I always find my way back," Katie admitted.

"Well, there you go! They probably think you'll show up any minute 'cuz that's what you always do, Katie! Now, chin up! Let's turn that frown upside down," Hoagie coaxed. He had heard the adult humans say that many times to the children, and it seemed to help. He was relieved to see that Katie was beginning to calm down. He crawled up on her head, and tried to wipe her tears with his teensy paw.

At that moment, Hoagie heard what sounded like two huge sniffs together. He had learned not to squeak when he was frightened, but he immediately ran underneath Katie's body to take shelter. Hoagie was trembling with fear until they heard a familiar voice croaking behind a bush.

"If we can just get through this mess of brambles, I'm sure we'll be able to see them." It was Felipa, the old frog, and behind her were two gigantic capybaras! Hoagie almost fainted despite himself. To him, they looked like massive, hairy monsters!

"Mama?! Dada!!" Katie exclaimed, running to them and leaving Hoagie exposed in the sunlight alone. "You came for me!! You do miss me!!" Katie was overjoyed, and the three capybaras started snuggling and chirping joyfully together.

While Hoagie was very happy for Katie, he couldn't help but feel a little abandoned, for now he would have to travel alone. Lately, he'd started becoming rather fond of Katie, and he'd gotten used to having a friend around. He didn't really know what to do next, or where to go. He knew he wouldn't be able to swim back to the main forest they had come from, and he didn't want to stay on the island, especially with all those toxic frogs. He would be alone again.

Oh, well, he thought, *it's not like I haven't been alone before...I'm used to it, right?* He also knew that he was the smartest hamster on this island (the *only* hamster, but still...), and he was determined to figure this problem out. He gave one last quick look at Katie and her nuzzling family, and started to make his way across the sand. Maybe if he was lucky, he could hitch a ride on Flamingo Joe's back.

"Hoagie!! Where you going? Silly, come back here!" Katie ran up to Hoagie and was jumping all around him like a hot potato. "Come and meet my mom and dad! I told them all about you, and they can't wait to meet you. They even said that if you're really as awesome as I say you are, you can come and live with us if you want to!! You, me, and my whole familia!"

Hoagie's teensy mouth dropped open in disbelief. Did he really hear Katie right? He would never have to live in the forest all alone, after all? It seemed too good to be true! He would never have to be stuck in a big purple ball ever again!

He would never have to sit in a cage that made his little feet hurt! And he'd be able to pig out on all the worms he ever wanted!

Hoagie knew he was a little sassy at times, and arrogant, and people might even think he was somewhat rude. Could he really be a part of a group, a big family, with friends to play with, and talk to, and sing with? He was worried that people wouldn't like him. But what did all that matter, anyway? Katie liked him, Flamingo Joe liked him, and even Felipa liked him. That's all that really mattered to him.

Hoagie turned to Katie's parents and, with the hugest grin on his face, stood on his little hind legs and announced, "Call me Hoagie, the smallest capybara to ever walk the face of the earth! That's right, I said *smallest*, and you know what? I don't even care about being small, or plump, or *pretty*, for that matter! People seem to like me just the way that I am, and that's fine with me!" Hoagie bowed dramatically, then sang, in what he thought was a terrific voice, "Let's go home!"

Thus ended Katie and Hoagie's first adventure, and started their long and wonderful friendship.

CPSIA information can be obtained
at www.ICGtesting.com
Printed in the USA
BVOW05*0324251116
468755BV00013B/36/P